An Actor's Life for Me!

So I wish you first a
Sense of theatre; only
Those who love illusion
    And know it will go far:
Otherwise we spend our
Lives in a confusion
Of what we say and do with
    Who we really are.

    —W. H. Auden,
      "Many Happy Returns"

An Actor's Life for Me!

LILLIAN GISH

AS TOLD TO SELMA G. LANES

ILLUSTRATIONS BY PATRICIA HENDERSON LINCOLN

Viking Kestrel

The authors acknowledge that
a valuable source for this book was
Lillian Gish: The Movies, Mr. Griffith and Me!
by Lillian Gish and Ann Pinchot.

In memory of Dorothy   L. G.

For Lily Whiteman Gordon   S. G. L.

VIKING KESTREL
Published by the Penguin Group
A division of Penguin Books USA Inc.,
375 Hudson Street, New York, New York 10014, U.S.A.
Penguin Books Ltd, 27 Wrights Lane, London W8 5TZ, England
Penguin Books Australia Ltd, Ringwood, Victoria, Australia
Penguin Books Canada Ltd, 10 Alcorn Avenue, Toronto, Ontario, Canada M4V 3B2
Penguin Books (N.Z.) Ltd, 182-190 Wairau Road, Auckland 10, New Zealand

Penguin Books Ltd, Registered Offices: Harmondsworth, Middlesex, England

Text copyright © Lillian Gish and Selma Lanes, 1987
Illustrations copyright © Patricia Henderson Lincoln, 1987
All rights reserved

First published in 1987 by Viking Penguin Inc.
Published simultaneously in Canada

Printed in United States of America
by Rae Publishing Co., Inc., Cedar Grove, New Jersey
Set in Times Roman.

2   3   4   5   6   7   8   9   10

Library of Congress Cataloging in Publication Data
Gish, Lillian, 1896–   An actor's life for me.
Summary: Covers Lillian Gish's childhood years, spent in
the theater in the early 1900s before the movie era.
1. Gish, Lillian, 1896–   —Childhood and youth—
Juvenile literature.   2. Actors—United States—
Biography—Juvenile literature.   [1. Gish, Lillian, 1896–
—Childhood and youth.   2. Actors and actresses]
I. Lanes, Selma G.   II. Title.
PN2287.G55A3   1987   791.43′028′0924   [B]   [92]   87-8197   ISBN 0-670-80416-9

Contents

CHAPTER ONE

Introducing Me and My First Play

Mrs. Gish with Baby Lillian

I am Lillian Diana Gish. I was named that by my parents. But sometimes I was called Florence Niles, Baby Alice, Baby Ann, and just plain Herself, for reasons that I will explain.

My sister Dorothy (who was nicknamed Doatsie) and I were lucky. We never lived in just one place or went to school like other children we knew. From the time I was six and Doatsie just four and a half, we were child actors. We belonged to traveling theatrical companies that performed plays in small towns and big cities all along the East Coast and in the Middle West.

There was no television, movies, or even radio at the beginning of this century when we began working. All over America, going to the theater was a popular evening entertainment. Most of the plays that Doatsie and I acted in were called melodramas.

A melodrama is a story with a beautiful heroine, a handsome hero, and a wicked villain. It was always the villain's job to make the heroine miserable. One of the best ways of doing this was to harm the heroine's young child, or maybe her baby sister. That's where Doatsie or I came in. Every melodrama ended with the handsome hero outsmarting the villain. But no one could ever be absolutely sure of this until the curtain fell at the play's end.

While most children our age were having lessons in classrooms five days a week, we were traveling in the day coaches of railroad trains between one small-town theater and the next. And while most children were sleeping soundly in their beds at home, we were jouncing along on milk trains in the small hours of the morning, moving on to some distant city on our schedule of performances.

If our acting company was having a good year, this wandering life could go on for as many as forty weeks. When that happened, my sister and I would earn enough money to keep our small family—Mother, Doatsie, and I—together over the summer when all the theaters were closed.

Perhaps this sounds exciting, like running away to join the circus or being carried off by gypsies. But I was much too busy to think about my life at the time. Traveling and acting, then traveling again, were everyday things to me. I am going to tell you about the actor's life—my own—and what it was like to be a child in the American theater at the beginning of this century, from approximately 1902 to 1912.

The only acting lesson I ever had came from the stage manager of my very first play, a melodrama called *In Convict Stripes*. "Little girl," he shouted, "speak loud and clear, or we'll get another little girl." I spoke loud and clear.

I was playing the part of Mabel Payne, the beautiful heroine's small daughter. You can be sure I was in for lots of trouble from the villain of the play.

My big scene came during the third act. The setting was a stone quarry. The villain was planning to kill Mabel—me!—by dynamiting the place. What he didn't know was that the hero, just offstage, was preparing to swing across the quarry by rope and scoop me up in his strong arms just seconds before the explosion took place.

It wasn't possible to use a real child for so dramatic a rescue. After all, the hero was just another actor, not a trapeze artist. Instead, a dummy dressed exactly like me would be substituted. During the excitement caused by the explosion, I was supposed to run behind a large papier-mâché rock and keep myself hidden from the audience.

We practiced that play for long hours and days in New York City before starting out on tour. Every time we rehearsed my scene, one of the actors would shout "Boom!" to let us know the explosion was taking place. That was my signal to creep behind the fake boulder and disappear from the audience's view.

In Convict Stripes opened in the small town of Risingsun, Ohio. The theater was a made-over barn, with the audience sitting on long wooden benches. When my big moment came in act III, I was ready. But I wasn't in any way ready for the genuine-sounding stage explosion that took place. It shook the barn rafters. Terrified, I forgot everything I had so carefully rehearsed. I ran screaming off the stage in one direction, while the hero, clutching my dummy substitute, swung to safety in the other.

The audience burst out laughing at this unexpected slapstick climax.

I felt disgraced and hid. The stage manager finally found me crouching behind a large cardboard box under the stage. I was coaxed out for curtain calls, sitting on the shoulders of the play's handsome hero, Walter Huston. (He later became a star of both silent films and talking pictures.)

From that night on, I stuffed my ears with cotton so as not to hear that awful stage explosion. But the incident taught me something about acting on stage. The explosion frightened me because it had sounded so real. But didn't that mean that the actor's job was to sound real, too? As Mabel Payne, I should sound and look as frightened as I had been when I ran off the stage. Acting wasn't just a game of learning lines and saying them at the right time.

For my first performance in Risingsun, I was listed on the program as Baby Lillian. In other places that season I was billed as Herself, which was the way a dog or cat was alway credited on playbills!

There was another reason that I never forgot *In Convict Stripes*. One night, in Dayton, Ohio, the actor playing the part of a prison guard accidentally dropped his gun. It went off. Though it was loaded only with buckshot, one of my legs was peppered with painful powder burns. I ran offstage in great pain.

Luckily, there was a doctor in the audience. He examined my leg and decided I could continue in my part through the last act. When I came on stage again, the audience applauded.

After the final curtain, the doctor led me into the lobby. It was the best-lit place in the theater. He sat me in a deep plush chair. Then, with a long needle, he pried out the bits of buckshot. Though it hurt a lot, I didn't cry. Actors must conceal their private feelings in public. I wasn't quite sure whether it was Mabel Payne or me who was hurting. I was learning my job!

The Dayton newspapers carried a story about my accident. When Grandfather McConnell (Mother's father), who lived nearby, saw it, he sent her the clipping. He never approved of his grandchildren acting on the stage, so he wanted to make sure that his daughter saw just what sort of life her children were leading, and how they were suffering as a result.

The accident had a happier side. When my Great-aunt Carrie and Uncle Homer read the same news story, they sent me a wonderful consolation present: a feather-soft fur neckpiece and matching muff. The muff had a small secret pocketbook tucked inside its midsection. Both pieces were made of pale-beige lamb's wool. I loved them more than any other possession I carried in my small suitcase.

When I got back to New York many months later, I found out that Doatsie had had her own troubles that first season on the road. She played the role of Little Willie in a play called *East Lynne*. In the last act, Little Willie dies and must lie dead on a bench, while several adults stand about conversing. One night, Dorothy fell fast asleep and rolled off the bench onto the stage. It broke up the performance.

Being an actor isn't an easy job.

CHAPTER TWO

How Mother, Doatsie, and I Went on the Stage

James and Mary McConnell Gish

I began life in Springfield, Ohio. I was born in my Grandmother Gish's house in October 1896.

The nicest thing I remember about Mother and Father together is seeing them both standing at the foot of my bed one night, when I was still quite small. Mother was wearing a red satin dress with a long train and Father had on a dark, elegant suit. They must have been going to a party. They both looked so beautiful that the image has always stayed in my mind, clear as a photograph in a family album. Surely they were happy then.

When my sister Dorothy was just a baby, Father would sometimes take me for walks. I was not yet three, and we would stop to rest and have some refreshment. We never stopped at an ice-cream parlor, always at a saloon. I remember the wood walls, the sawdust on the floor and the strange bitter smell. Father loved to show me off. While he stood drinking beer, he would lift me up onto the bar, where I sat and ate my fill of the free lunch—usually baked beans and sour pickles. I don't think these walks, or their destination, pleased Mother, but she never said anything.

Mother made all my clothes, and I liked showing them off. Our Grandfather McConnell had a harness and saddle shop in Dayton, Ohio. Whenever we visited him, Grandfather would lift me onto the magnificent stuffed horse that stood in the store's front window. I would sit proud and straight in the saddle, my lace-trimmed petticoat and skirt billowing over my spindly legs. It was a treat I dearly loved.

Father never stayed in one place for long. By the time I was four, we had moved from Springfield to Dayton, Ohio, and then to Baltimore, Maryland. Father was a confectioner—he made candy and sold it in his own store.

Not long after we had settled in Baltimore, Father decided that New York was a much better place to make his fortune. Leaving Mother behind in Baltimore with us, he went there alone to find a job and a place for us to live.

One day, Mother got tired of just waiting in Baltimore for news from Father. She packed us up, and we too left for New York.

Mother rented a flat on Eighth Avenue at 28th Street. She also got a job in a Brooklyn department store and bought furniture for us, on "time." This meant that she had to pay a small sum of money every week until it was all paid for.

Father lived with us at first. He stayed at home taking care of Dorothy and me. Every Friday a bushy-browed man known only as The Collector came by for the furniture money—three dollars. Mother always left that sum with Father just before going to work.

One day, as Dorothy and I sat cutting paper dolls at the dining room table, two big men arrived instead of The Collector. They took our bedroom furniture away.

Father had put the furniture money to some other use. Soon afterward, Father disappeared from our lives—but not completely. During the next few years he sometimes turned up and talked of coming back so that we could be a whole family again. But Mother had tried too many times to be tempted. Sometimes he wanted to take one of us away with him. That scared us.

Our greatest fear was of being separated from Mother. She gave us security. Father brought us insecurity. As I grew older, I often wondered which was the more valuable gift. Insecurity taught me to work as if everything depended on me, and to pray as if everything depended on God. Somehow, given enough insecurity, I learned to do for myself, never counting on others to do things for me. Wherever Mother was, we had love, peace, and sympathy. Yet, without the insecurity Father brought, the blessings Mother provided might have left us weak, dependent, and helpless.

When we came to New York, the Flatiron Building at Twenty-third Street and Fifth Avenue was the tallest building in the city. We were so poor that we couldn't even afford the nickel it cost to ride the streetcars. On Sundays Mother would dress us in our going-out best—with hats—and we would walk from our apartment to the Flatiron Building.

Even on a still day the winds around the building were fierce. So Dorothy and I invented a wonderful game: The object was to keep our hats on our heads and, at the same time, keep our skirts down where they belonged. It was a pretty fancy balancing act. If you concentrated on holding your skirt in place using two hands, your hat was sure to take off down Fifth Avenue. But if you made the mistake of clutching your hat with both hands, your skirt and petticoats would fly up over your face. It was an exciting challenge!

When Father left, Mother took in two young actresses as boarders. It helped pay the rent. One night one of them, Dolores Lorne, tried to advise my mother.

"Mary, you work for so little money," she said. "With your good looks, you could be on the stage. And with any luck, you'll do well and be able to educate your children properly."

Soon Mother did get work as an actress—with Proctor's Stock Company. The pay was fifteen dollars a week. She tucked us into bed each night before going off to the theater for her evening performances. Neighbors looked in on us from time to time. I still remember the mattress on the floor beside our bed, in case we fell out while Mother was gone.

On matinee days Mother took us with her to the theater. Doatsie and I played quietly in the dressing room while she was on stage.

One afternoon an actress friend, Alice Niles, came backstage to talk with Mother. She had been offered a leading part in a touring company.

"The only hitch," she said, "is that I must find a little girl to play my daughter. Lillian is just about the right age." I was almost six.

Mother didn't like the idea one bit. Alice Niles said that my salary would be ten dollars a week and that the tour might last forty weeks. A child could live easily on three dollars a week. My savings could help tide us over the long summer, when Proctor's would be closed.

She promised Mother to care for me as if I were her own child. Surely I would be safe with "Aunt" Alice. Finally, Mother agreed.

Soon after I went "on the road" with Alice Niles in *In Convict Stripes,* Mother wrote to tell me that Dolores Lorne had taken Doatsie on tour with her in *East Lynne.* Doatsie got fifteen dollars a week! Hers was a bigger company playing in larger cities than mine.

In this way, without ever intending to, Mother, Doatsie, and I all became play actors in the same year—1902.

CHAPTER THREE

The Awe-Inspiring Rescue of a Child

Dorothy and Lillian Gish

After my first season on tour, I always prayed that Mother, Dorothy, and I might be in a company together. That very autumn, my hopes were realized. The three of us were hired for a touring troupe of *Her First False Step.* Our combined pay was forty-five dollars a week!

Though she was almost five, Dorothy played a babe in arms, carried onstage by the heroine in act one. Helen Ray, the star of *Her First False Step,* told us many years later, "I had a long speech to give with Dorothy sitting on my lap. But I could never keep her from looking out at the audience and distracting everyone. When I found out how much she loved black jelly beans, I would lay three out on the table beside us at each performance. I told her she could eat them at the end of the act if only she would keep looking straight at them. The trick worked almost every time, and it saved my speech."

I was the older child, out barefoot in the snow peddling newspapers. "Papers—*World* and *Evening Journal!*" was one of my longer lines.

The "snow" was made of cut-up paper, which the stage crew swept up at the end of each performance to be used again. Sometimes bits of wood and nails—once even a small dead mouse—fell on me along with the paper flakes.

Her First False Step was another melodrama. Again, my big moment came in the third act. The setting was a circus. This time the villain threw me into the lions' cage. The hero, of course, dived in to rescue me.

Mother, who had just a small part, was not at all happy about my scene in the lions' cage. But I liked it. I had never been to a circus or met a lion before, but I loved all animals.

The lions, Teddy and Jenny, and their trainer were part of the traveling company. They really came from a circus and had never been declawed. During rehearsals, I found out that a fine wire-screen would separate me from the lions. It was so fine that it was invisible from even a few feet away.

Sometimes women in the audience fainted when the villain tossed me into the cage. As soon as the lion tamer (dressed exactly like the hero) rushed in and saved me, the screen would be pulled back. Then he would chase the lions back and forth till the curtain fell.

During that season Jenny gave birth to a cub. Dorothy and I treated it like a kitten. We loved to play with the tawny little thing. When the cub was no more than a few weeks old, it was sent ahead of the company to the next town on our tour—as an advertisement for the coming theatrical attraction. People were urged to come "see the awe-inspiring rescue of a child from savage African lions." In one town the cub was put in the window of a shoe store. It gnawed through thirty-eight dollars' worth of slippers, using them as teething rings!

At matinees the audience would be invited to stay in their seats during intermission, while Dorothy and I fed meat to the cub's parents on the ends of long poles.

When we played in Philadelphia, a group of newsboys came to a performance. They hissed at the villain and cheered for the hero and this small heroine. The next evening two of the boys came to the stage door to give Dorothy and me a small bottle of perfume. We were thrilled. Nothing like this had ever happened to us before.

In order to cut expenses the following season, the company took only one child on tour. Dorothy stayed in the cast, and I got another job as the younger sister in a melodrama called *The Child Wife.*

During one happy week our two troupes crossed paths. We played in the same town at the same time. Our matinees were on different days, so I had a chance to be with Mother and Dorothy during their afternoon performance. I couldn't bear to watch Dorothy during the circus scene. I rushed back to the dressing room and put a pillow over my head in order to shut out the terrible sound of the roaring lions.

My fear wasn't exactly groundless. After the lions went back to their real-life circus, Jenny tore off her trainer's arm!

CHAPTER FOUR

An Actor's Life for Me

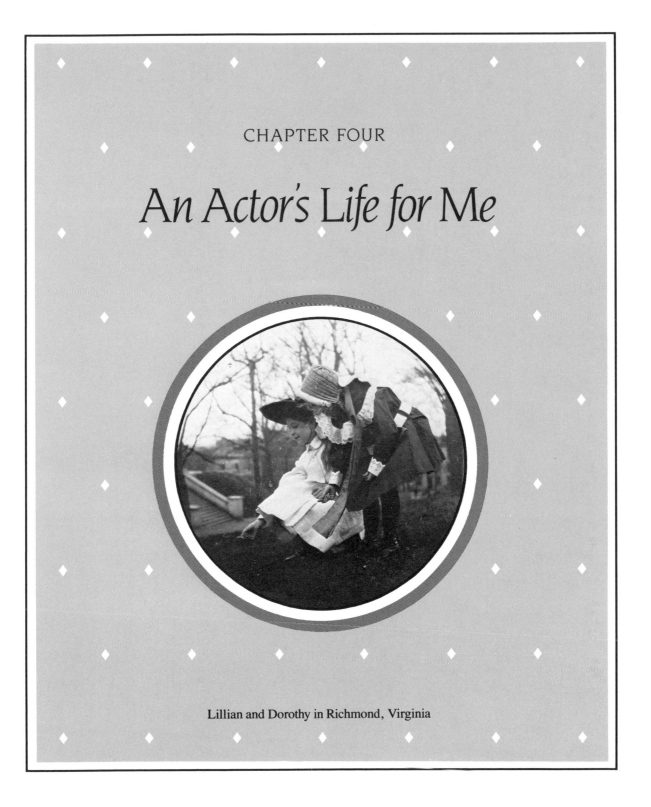

Lillian and Dorothy in Richmond, Virginia

Mother and Dorothy often were together on the road, acting in one company while I was far away traveling with another. Younger than me by almost two years, Doatsie was less able to be on her own. I could take care of myself.

As the trains I rode on sped past towns, with crossing gates lowered and warning bells clanging, I would press my nose to the window and watch for the little white church, the schoolhouse, the scattered stores and homes. I would tell myself how lucky I was to be on the road. I even tried to believe it.

Between towns I would stare out the window and just daydream. I tried not to think too much about Mother and Dorothy, or about what they might be doing. Thoughts like those hurt. Instead, I would try to think about our summers together in Massillon, Ohio, where we stayed with Mother's sister, Aunt Emily. I thought of the front porch there, of the cat and dog. I thought of our cousins who had given Dorothy her nickname, Doatsie. I thought of the pleasure of hauling new-mown grass in a little red wagon. Sometimes we even went to school there during the summer session.

I wondered what it would be like to be grownup, to have enough money to live in a beautiful house with Mother and Dorothy. When I was lucky, after thoughts like these faded, I'd be left with a lovely, peaceful feeling. If Aunt Alice Niles or some other theater "aunt" asked me what I was looking at so hard and so long, I'd always answer, "Nothing . . . just looking."

On the road an actor's life was divided between performing and riding on trains. Usually trains were the only way to travel between the towns and cities that had booked our play. We performed on six nights and at two matinees every week.

No food was served either on the day coaches or late-night milk trains that we rode, so we ate whenever we could. During my first season, since Aunt Alice was a vegetarian, I ate mostly milk and oatmeal for five cents a serving. Often I ordered two portions of oatmeal for my dinner. This enabled me to live easily on three dollars a week. I sent seven dollars home to Mother every single week!

The distance between towns on our schedule was often short, and mostly we slept on the day coaches during the trip. Sometimes the trains carried us in and out of towns where we played for just a single night.

Whenever we reached a new town, Aunt Alice or another female player would take me with her to rent a room in a second-class hotel or, better, a rooming house. This would cost no more than fifty cents a day. Back then, actors were considered untrustworthy. In many hotel lobbies there was a sign reading NO DOGS OR ACTORS ALLOWED.

But the owners of boarding houses always looked kindly on what appeared to be a young mother traveling with her child.

As soon as Aunt Alice and I were settled in our room, the other ladies of the company, having left their luggage backstage at the theater, would come to call. They stayed for the entire day and shared the cost of the room with us.

I see them still, lying crosswise on the bed asleep, or perhaps sewing, or just talking. If there was hot water—a rare luxury—we could bathe and wash our stockings.

I would curl up in a chair or, if I wasn't tired, take a walk by myself. I loved to watch children playing. It was more exciting to me than the best melodrama. Because we were with adults so much of the time, both Dorothy and I grew up too fast. I had no idea what to say to another child my own age. I was sensible and responsible, but I never did learn how to play.

Once when I was out walking I saw a long line of people filing into a church. I wondered what could be happening and got in line, too. At the end, I found only a plain wooden box. Inside it was the first dead person I ever saw! Holding back a scream, I ran outside. Never again did I stand in any line unless I knew exactly what I'd find at the other end.

We always gave up our rented room just before the evening performance. Usually we took the very next train out of town—it saved on hotel bills. Sometimes, we had a long wait at the depot. Then, the men of the company would take off their overcoats and make bedding for me. The bed itself would sometimes be the sloping desk used for writing telegrams—if the stationmaster was the sort who took pity on a small, weary trouper. One of the actors always stood guard to make sure I didn't roll off.

If the waiting room had wooden benches with armrests every few feet, I could slip under the armrests, stretch out full length and fall right asleep. I remember how sorry everyone was when, at about the age of nine, I outgrew this sort of makeshift bed. Then I'd nap on the stone waiting-room floors, with newspapers under my body. Like soldiers on the march, actors quickly learn how to fall asleep anywhere.

The worst thing that ever happened to me on tour happened my first year on the road. One winter night, Aunt Alice and I were running across a small footbridge to catch the milk train to our next stop. I clutched the small traveling case containing all my belongings. In my hurry to get ready, I must have been careless about fastening the straps. They came undone on the bridge, and all my precious possessions tumbled out and into the fast-moving stream below. Everything—including my beautiful fur piece and muff—was lost. To try to rescue even a single item would have meant missing the train. I ran on, hardly looking back, the open bag flapping at my side. Now I had no spare underwear, stockings, or even a nightdress. It was a dreadful loss. No money was sent home to Mother that sad week.

Money was always a concern among actors on tour. The theater company paid only train fare, in addition to salary. Every other expense, including room and board, was our own.

Somtimes, if the tour manager was dishonest or the play unsuccessful, a company would run out of funds. More than once, we would

be stranded in mid-season far away from New York. In order to survive such a calamity, traveling players sometimes had to steal away from a hotel or boarding house in the middle of the night, leaving unpaid bills behind. I came to understand that terrible sign: NO DOGS OR ACTORS ALLOWED.

In any traveling troupe, the actors soon became one big family—at least for the season. By the time we had been on the road for a month, stagehands, bit-part players, and stars were all old friends. Accepted as equals, children got both affection and protection.

I learned to read that first year on the road, because the actors read so patiently and beautifully from my copy of *Black Beauty* whenever I asked. Soon I knew each page by heart; then the words began to make sense, too.

For Dorothy and me the stage was our school, our home, and our entire life for most of the years of our childhood. The parts we played were always sad ones. No sadder than our own lives, many grownups might think. But Doatsie and I thought we were lucky, always to be seeing new places and meeting new people. It wasn't until I was almost grown-up that I thought how odd it was: We were keeping our family together by being apart for at least half of every year!

Whenever I did travel with Mother and Dorothy, Mother treated our route as if it were a course in the geography and history of the United States. Were we going to Boston this trip? Then she would have a book about the Pilgrims with her. If there was time, she would take us to Plymouth Rock.

Once, when we were down South, in Chattanooga, she told us about her uncle, a Captain McConnell, who had fought with the

Union Army during the Civil War and had died near there. We had time that trip for a ride up Lookout Mountain. Imagine how proud we were to come upon a stone marker with that very uncle's name on it, citing his valor in battle!

Mother liked to have us visit factories in the towns where we played. In Durham, North Carolina, we rode to the end of the trolley line to see a tobacco factory. A beautiful black woman stopped her machine and gave Dorothy and me a cigarette three feet long! She coiled it into a box for us as a souvenir. In another town, we rode a streetcar out to see the cotton fields in bloom.

Mother's favorite places for study were graveyards. We always looked for gravestones with family names like Barnard and Robinson. On Mother's side of the family, we could trace our ancestry back to some of the earliest settlers. President Zachary Taylor was a relative, too. It surprised us to see how many times familiar names turned up, but, of course, this country was a lot younger then. Mother's great-great-grandmother shook hands with President George Washington when she was a little girl!

Traveling from one town to another in winter, we were often cold and sometimes hungry. But dirt bothered me the most. In some hotels and boardinghouses the rooms were encrusted with filth, with bugs and cockroaches. If we were going to be in a room long enough, Mother would scour it. I remember one particularly cold and shabby room with leaking walls and the smell of decay everywhere. When I said my prayers that night, I had a special last sentence: "Please God, don't let us wake up in the morning."

This wasn't as terrible as it sounds. I never doubted that the three of us would all be in heaven together—forever—when we died. I guess I felt a little like the writer of one of the gravestone inscriptions we had read: "I do not mourn the good who die / For goodness has a place on high." Mother had always brought us up to be polite and good, so we fully expected heaven to be our reward.

We had our favorite cities. We loved to play in Norfolk and in Richmond, because there were boardinghouses there that served ham and chicken—at the same meal! And they had sweet potatoes and either gingerbread or pecan pie as well. In the Middle West, we always hoped to play in towns where there was a church supper. You could pay your quarter entrance fee and stuff yourself to the bursting point. The parishioners watched us, wide-eyed. I don't think they had ever seen children eat so much.

We liked Philadelphia, too. As soon as we settled in there, usually for a few days' stay, we would rush out to the Automat with three or four nickels in hand. It was the delight of Doatsie's heart and mine to watch the foods we were about to eat doing pirouettes behind their little glass doors.

But our favorite city, without doubt, was New Haven, Connecticut. There, in the backstage corridor that led to our dressing room, was a small, sliding wooden panel at window level. On the far side of it was an ice-cream parlor! When you knocked twice at this magic portal, it slid open, and a chocolate ice-cream soda would be handed through. How wondrous that seemed to us. Ali Baba could not have cried "Open Sesame!" with any greater joy.

An Actor's Life for Me!

Sometimes, traveling *with* Mother had more dreadful moments than traveling alone. There was the time that Doatsie, at age seven, came down with scarlet fever in a hotel in Scranton, Pennsylvania. It wasn't a bad case, but in those days local boards of health posted quarantine signs on your door as soon as a case was reported. Afraid that we might all be quarantined, our company fled at once, taking me with them. At least one child was absolutely necessary for our next performance.

As it happened, the hotel faced the Scranton railroad station platform. It was elevated, so I could look across and see Mother standing at the hotel room window. Oh, the pain of waiting for that train to carry me away from Dorothy and Mother. I remember waving goodbye and feeling certain my heart would break.

My first Christmas away from Mother and Dorothy was in Detroit, Michigan, where there was an automobile showroom near the stage door. After the Christmas-day matinee, I noticed a lighted tree in the showroom window. I was sure it hadn't been there before.

Underneath it, as if by some miracle, were all the items I had asked of Santa Claus in a confidential letter a week or so earlier: a sled, a little comb, brush and mirror set, and a furpiece and muff almost exactly like the ones I had lost in the stream! As I stood there open-mouthed, three men came out of the showroom. "Lillian," one said, "we thought you'd never come. Santa left these presents for you." Oh, beautiful world, and how kind its people.

Whenever anyone mentions Detroit, I think of those three strangers who, with the help of our generous company, went to such trouble to make a child's Christmas day so happy.

For the rest of that winter, uncomplaining, our traveling troupe carried the sled along with us. If there were snow enough, I was pulled to and from the theater, like some Arctic queen.

CHAPTER FIVE

A Christmas Like No Other

The Gish sisters

One special Christmas fell on a Sunday, a traveling Sunday. The manager of our troupe, a Mr. Schiller, had made arrangements for the company to move to our next town by freight train.

All of us rode in the train's last car—the caboose. It was the only car with seats, even if they were uncomfortable, hard wooden benches along the sides of the car. This caboose happened to be damp and dirty. And it got damper and dirtier each time one of the trainmen threw open the door, letting in a blast of bitter-cold air and stamping his snowy boots on the already muddy floor.

Dorothy and I seldom knew what day of the week it was or even if it was a holiday. Our schedule never changed: We were either acting, or traveling between acting engagements. Sometimes we didn't get to sleep in a real bed for nights on end.

As the freight train bump-bumped along, shaking up everyone's insides, the company huddled together, vibrating in unison inside that dingy, ill-lit caboose.

At last we came to a stop in what looked like a big town. With a freight train, there was going to be a lot of backing and switching before getting under way again. Since this took a while, most members of the company left the car and went into town. Somehow Dorothy and I fell asleep while they were gone.

When we awakened, the train was moving, and in the middle of that dreary little caboose stood a small green Christmas tree. It smelled of fresh pine and was decorated with popcorn balls and candy canes. There were two oranges apiece for us, too, with lemon sticks to suck the juice through. This was Dorothy's and my favorite treat in the whole world!

We were certain that Santa Claus himself had managed to find us out there. How clever of him! Only years later did we realize how the tree came to be where it was. Though actors had little spare cash for frivolities, they were often extraordinarily generous to children in the troupe. In those days, a tree probably cost ten or fifteen cents, and it would have taken a quarter or more to decorate it so beautifully—not negligible sums back then.

I never see a caboose or read about one now without recalling that beautiful Christmas surprise so many years ago.

CHAPTER SIX

Mother

Mrs. Gish

Mother was always worrying about Dorothy and me. She spent most of her spare time doing things for us. We might go hungry now and then, but our underwear was always hand-trimmed with fine lace. All the clothes we wore were made by her. She seemed never to sew for herself.

Every summer in Ohio she went through the pattern books and used Aunt Emily's sewing machine to make us new outfits for the coming season. Doatsie and I had identical wardrobes: one coat, one good dress, and one everyday dress. Mother's skill as a seamstress contributed a lot to our appearance. I remember how much the company of *Her First False Step* admired the little black velveteen coat she made for me that year.

When I grew up, I once asked Mother why she had never remarried.

"I wasn't sure another father would be good to you children," she said.

I also wondered why Mother had not simply gone home to Grandfather McConnell's big house in Ohio when she and Father parted. Grandfather was a prosperous widower. He could easily have cared for us. The answer, I decided, was that she wanted to do something purposeful and responsible with her own life, as well as to provide for her children. Pride demanded that she—and we—succeed on our own.

Just about the only thing that bothered Dorothy and me about Mother was the way she never answered any question with a simple Yes or No, like other parents. If we asked, "Can we do this?" "May we try that?" Mother always answered, "If you think it's the right thing to do." She knew we were frequently on our own, away from her good counsel. So she tried to help us learn to think for ourselves.

Mother liked good manners in children—in grownups, too. "I suppose you can get through life without manners," she'd say. "But how much pleasanter for you and everybody else when you behave well."

One spring we were all in New York at Easter time. Doatsie begged Mother to make herself a new dress. Finally she gave in and bought some soft silken cloth, blue as the sky on a summer's day. She made a lovely Empire-style dress. Then she bought a hat frame in the dime store and covered it with tiny pink cloth roses.

Mother looked so pretty in her new outfit. We could hardly wait for Easter Sunday when she promised to wear it to church. Meanwhile, the blue dress hung in the closet, with the hat carefully placed on the shelf above it.

That spring we lived on the top floor of a rooming house. When Dorothy and I were falling asleep, we often heard the sound of rain pattering on the roof.

On Easter Sunday, Mother opened the closet. A steady leak was dripping down from the ceiling, dripping directly onto Mother's lovely hat with the pink roses! And the roses were dripping directly onto Mother's beautiful blue dress. It was badly stained—ruined. How my sister and I both wailed!

As usual, Mother comforted us. We were all three together, weren't we? And it was a lovely Easter Sunday, wasn't it? Mother was the Great Comforter of our childhood. She never fretted about what couldn't be changed. She always did whatever she could to make the burdens of life fall more lightly on Dorothy and me.

Being with Mother, and thinking about her when we were apart, gave our gypsy-like childhood whatever lasting beauty it had.

CHAPTER SEVEN

Summertime

Dorothy in *Her First False Step*

After our traveling seasons in the theater, we usually spent the summer in Massillon with Mother's younger sister Emily. Though we all worked hard, still there was seldom quite enough money to keep the three of us in New York.

Mother would carefully scrape any labels off our luggage. No one back home in Ohio must suspect that we were on the stage. When we were young, the only time a lady had her name in the papers was when she married and when she died. Actors broke that rule. Once we were in Massillon, Aunt Emily reminded us daily not to tell anyone in town about our life in the theater. If we did, she said, parents would not let their children play with us.

When we returned to New York in the fall, we always made the rounds of the agencies that specialized in jobs for children. We learned to arrive at an agency early—about eight in the morning. Then we were able to stake a place right by the door. In this way, the producer, who usually arrived about ten, would be sure to see us. If by luck we were chosen, we were called into another room to audition for the play's manager.

Making the rounds, Mother became good friends with another mother of theater children: Mrs. Charlotte Smith. She had three children to support—Gladys, Lotte, and Jack. How we loved the Smiths, particularly Gladys, the eldest. Little did any of us dream that, under a different name, she would become world-famous.

After our second season, the Smiths shared a railroad flat with us from April through September. It cut expenses and was fun for us all. Mother taught Mrs. Smith how to sew; and Dorothy and Jack, who were nearly the same age, had grand times together. Gladys, who was nine and older than I was by about a year, would take all of us to the theater on matinee days.

As theatrical children, we had professional cards giving our names and the name of the most recent play we had toured in. If we showed these at the box office, and if there were empty seats, the attendant would "recognize professionals." That meant we got free seats!

Usually the five of us climbed high up into the gallery. "Now listen carefully to the way the actors speak," Gladys would instruct us. "Watch everything they do. Maybe someday we will play on Broadway."

After the second season of *Her First False Step,* Mother managed to save enough money to open a candy and popcorn stand at the Fort George Amusement Park. It was at the northern tip of Manhattan. We took the streetcar there from our apartment every day. The Smiths didn't live with us that summer, but they often came to visit us at Fort George.

Mother had hired a man to make the taffy, and we children would wrap it. Our motto was, "Wrap one, eat two."

The job we loved best that summer was standing on a box and calling out to the crowd to come and taste our wares. We lined up for turns.

"Where's Dorothy?" Mother asked one afternoon when we were all calling customers. Neither the Smiths nor I could tell her. "She was here just a while ago," Jack said. "I didn't see her leave."

Mother looked around the nearby stands, then began to walk farther away. Finally, almost frantic, she spotted Dorothy's face. She was standing high up on the snake charmer's platform. Mother pushed her way through an admiring crowd. She nearly fainted when she saw her younger daughter full length.

There she was, an enormous snake curled around her. It nearly covered her small body. Dorothy stood smiling and fearless, basking in the admiration and awe of her audience.

For the rest of that day an unhappy Dorothy had to sit under our stand, missing her turns at both taffy wrapping and crowd calling.

Though Dorothy was the younger, and sometimes quite foolish, I admired her greatly. I was the family worrier. Was I good enough? Was I trying hard enough? Dorothy was full of fun, fearless, and always willing to take a chance on new experiences. Dorothy was the side of me that God had left out.

That summer at Fort George, Dorothy and I discovered the delights of Potatoes Anna—thin potato slices browned in butter in a big iron skillet. Whenever we earned a nickel, we spent it on them.

There was also a Mr. Craemer and his pony concession. On rainy days, when there was no business at either Mother's stand or Mr. Craemer's, he would let Dorothy and me exercise the ponies, riding bareback. How we loved to race around the wet track, our hair loose and flying out behind us. We had only one accident, but that was a bad one. Dorothy's pony stumbled and fell, and she went over its head. She lay there in the mud absolutely still. Mr. Craemer called an ambulance and Mother rode with Dorothy to the hospital. Her arm had a compound fracture.

By the time Mother got back to Fort George, it was evening. No one had any idea where I had gone. People on the grounds had searched for me everywhere. Mother was clever enough to think of the machinery shed at the center of the merry-go-round. There she found me crouched, terrified. She took me in her arms and assured me that Dorothy was going to be all right. I had been certain she was dead and I wanted to die, too. Without Doatsie, life would have no laughter, no sunshine. It was unimaginable.

CHAPTER EIGHT

Dorothy's Broken Heart

Dorothy in the Fiske O'Hara Company

For three seasons Mother and Dorothy toured with Fiske O'Hara, a popular actor and producer of the time.

A handsome Irishman with a rich tenor voice, Mr. O'Hara always played the leading man in his own productions. Not only did he inspire dreams of romance in matinee audiences everywhere, but he won the heart of my sister Doatsie.

Under his spell Dorothy blossomed as an actor. A yellowed press clipping from 1907 reads:

> *Miss Dorothy Gish, who plays the part of Gillie, is one of the daintiest and sweetest little actresses seen here in a long time. Her work is admirable.*

Another reviewer was beguiled by her "flirtatious eyes."

At the time she fell in love, Doatsie was nine. Mr. O'Hara solemnly promised to wait for her to grow up. During perfomances Dorothy tried to keep her adored one in view. In their play that season she appeared in the last act wearing her nightgown. Usually she could stand in the wings and, awaiting her cue to go on stage, watch Mr O'Hara raptly. But if the theater was small, she couldn't quite see Mr. O'Hara from the wings.

At Stage Right in this play (the side from which Dorothy made her entrance), there was a fireplace. Its logs were lit by a red lightbulb. So mesmerized by Mr. O'Hara was Dorothy one night that, the better to see him, she crawled inside the fireplace and sat down on the logs. The red lightbulb glowed through her nightgown.

Unexpectedly, during the love scene, the audience began tittering. Mr. O'Hara quickly turned his back—were his pants properly buttoned? Then, looking wildly around the stage, he caught sight of Dorothy, dazed with love, glowing in the fireplace.

"Get the kid out of there!" he roared, and the play limped on toward its intended end.

The next season, while Doatsie and Mother were still in his company, Mr. O'Hara married his leading lady. I was traveling with another company, but Mother wrote: "I don't know what to do with Dorothy. Since the wedding she doesn't eat, just sits and daydreams. While I was dressing her for the second act last night, she fell right off the trunk as I was fastening her shoes."

In Dorothy's last play with Fiske O'Hara, she had another third act appearance. On Christmas Eve, Mr. O'Hara told Mother to keep the door of Dorothy's dressing room closed while he made a special announcement to the audience before the last act.

"We're changing the scene a bit tonight," he said, "and actually turning our set into Christmas Eve. It's a surprise for the child in our company. We'll have a lighted tree on stage that she knows nothing about. I hope you will enjoy with us whatever happens."

Mother wrote:

> *Dorothy went running onstage as usual, said her first line, then saw the tree. She almost stopped breathing, couldn't move or speak for the longest time. Then, bless her, she went right on with her lines, after kissing Mr. O'Hara on the cheek. The years of training, you see, pay highest dividends in an emergency.*

It had been drilled into us by Mother, and by every stage manager we ever worked with, that when an audience pays to see a performance, it is entitled to the best performance an actor can give. Nothing in one's own life—not fatigue or illness, not anxiety or even joy—must interfere.

CHAPTER NINE

The Gerry Men

Lillian with Nell Dorr, a Massillon friend

"If you don't behave, the Gerry men will get you! They'll lock you up in a big stone castle far away from your mother."

We heard versions of this threat many times. The Gerry men were a theater child's bogeyman. What a terrifying thought: to be separated from Mother permanently! I worried a lot about keeping out of the Gerry men's clutches.

By the end of the nineteenth century, the first child labor laws in this country had been passed. They protected poor children from hard and unhealthy work in mines, textile mills, sweatshops, and other factories. Often young children worked long hours under dangerous and unhealthy conditions. A verse of the time went:

> The golf course lies so near the mill
> That almost every day
> The working children can look out
> And see the men at play.

The Gerry Society was founded by Elbridge Thomas Gerry, a New York lawyer, who devoted much of his life to the protection of working children.

Somehow, by the early 1900s, the Gerry Society began to turn its watchful eye on children in the theater. Whether or not we or our parents wanted this attention, child players were singled out for rescue from gainful employment. No one seemed to care that we were leading busy, productive, and—on the whole—happy lives or that sometimes our wages helped to keep a family together.

For some reason the Society was particularly active in and around Chicago. Whenever we played in the Middle West, we had to be ready for the Gerry men to turn up without warning. Though Mother had taught us always to be truthful, this instance was an exception. We learned how to lie shamelessly, to camouflage immature bodies with long skirts, padding, grown-up shoes, and veils.

I was ten years old when I made my first appearance before a judge. Luckily, he accepted my high-heeled shoes, full-skirted dress, and hair swept up into a Psyche's knot as evidence of my being sixteen years old.

At about the same age Dorothy was taken alone into a judge's chambers. Mother waited anxiously outside while Dorothy was questioned behind closed doors. At last she came out, shaking her head from side to side.

"What a strange old gentleman!" she told Mother. "Do you know he didn't even know how many Commandments there were. I had to tell him!" Apparently the judge was sufficiently impressed by Dorothy's answers. He allowed her to continue acting, even at so tender an age.

Certainly our religious education was as good as any other child's. Whenever we were not traveling on Sunday, we were sent off to church—whatever church happened to be handy. We didn't mind, because every church was so different. Mother's family was Episcopalian, and Dorothy and I had been baptized and confirmed by the Bishop of Cleveland. But Mother believed that all religions were good and that any church was preferable to no church at all. Dorothy and I liked Catholic churches best. We couldn't understand a word of what was being said, but we loved all the bell ringing and the popping up and down in the pews. It was easily the most exciting service of all.

If anything, our lives were more sheltered than those of the children who went to school every day and lived in comfortable, secure houses with both their parents. We were constantly in the company of adults, and, as a rule, they were most particular about what they said in front of us. One of our stage carpenters once knocked a man down for cursing within my hearing.

As for the gypsy life we led, rattling about in drafty day coaches and on nearly empty milk trains up and down the Eastern Seaboard, there was something rather beautiful about it. Certainly, it taught us quite early to find joy in our work—one of the best lessons life has to offer. It is one that has served me well for more than eighty years.

CHAPTER TEN

I Go to Convent School

Lillian

I was ten years old and growing tall, fatal for a child actor. Jobs were harder to find. When the actress Maude Adams was casting for *Peter Pan,* I was taken to her dressing room at the Empire Theater for an interview. Miss Adams, a little woman herself, decided that a smaller child would be preferable in the role.

Mother foresaw this difficult time. In Ohio the previous summer she had wisely urged dancing lessons on me. My new skill proved useful almost immediately. Late that autumn I was chosen to dance in Sarah Bernhardt's company. The world-famous actress was embarking on the first of several "Farewell Tours" of America. She would perform at the Lyric Theater during a short New York engagement.

"The Divine Sarah" was no longer young. I remember her standing beside me in the wings one evening waiting for the curtain to rise. My hair was still very fair, and Mother put it up in curl papers every night. When she combed it out, the effect was like a halo around my face. Madame ran her fingers through my curls. I looked up at her, this strange, ghostly figure: dead-white face, frizzed red hair, and eyes the color of the sea. Her voice was like some lovely bird song. *"Ah, le petit ange aux beaux cheveux d'or,"* it chirped. I knew no French, but I learned later that it meant, "Ah, the little angel with beautiful golden hair."

For the first time in my life I was dancing on stage rather than speaking. How strange and confusing! It was my first time on Broadway, too. One thing really impressed me: the floors between the stage entrance and the dressing rooms were spread with canvas to protect our costumes. Also, there was always a maid backstage to press my costume—before every performance! And the discipline was rigid. As soon as I came offstage, another maid took me by the hand, whisked me up a long flight of stairs to the dressing room, helped me to change into my street clothes, then promptly ejected me out the stage door. This unfriendly efficiency bothered me—especially compared to the informality and camaraderie of our traveling companies.

When my dance role ended, Mother, Dorothy, and I got jobs in another melodrama, *At Duty's Call.* Our joy was short-lived as it proved to be a disaster. What we had always dreaded happened to us. We were stranded in a small Southern town without any pay and with no return tickets to New York! That winter was the low point of our stage careers. Poor Mother! She would have willingly starved to death herself rather than borrow money from Grandfather. But she could not bear to see us suffer. Finally, she wrote for a loan. Till then we had managed to get by on our own hard work and her thrift.

The lessons of that bleak time of cold, hunger, and discouragement lived on long in my heart.

People in other professions—teachers, librarians, even clerks in stores—have regular, weekly wages they can depend on. But the financial fate of actors—and all artists—is always precarious. I absorbed into my very bones Mother's economic philosophy: "If you can't pay cash, then better do without. It will help you to sleep at night." This became my eleventh commandment.

By the next summer Mother managed somehow to scrape together enough money to open an ice-cream parlor in East Saint Louis, near where her brother Henry Clay McConnell and his family lived. Dorothy went to Massillon as usual, but I went with Mother to help in the store.

Soon Mother decided that East Saint Louis was too rough a place for a young girl. She sent me instead to a nearby convent school, the Ursaline Academy.

Its protecting walls and peace and quiet appealed to me. I didn't even mind the strict rules. Wasn't I used to discipline from my theater travels? The students had to be up by five-thirty A.M., a bit early, but I loved the lessons, particularly French and music. And I loved the simple wholesome food. Also, I knew that Mother was paying the princely sum of twenty dollars a month to keep me there. I was determined to get her money's worth!

The Sisters knew nothing of my life on the stage. After summers in Massillon I knew better than to mention acting. I was afraid that if the Sisters learned the awful truth, I would be asked to leave the convent. Even after I was chosen to appear in a play, and then in an opera, I was determined to forget about being an actor. I chose a new career: I was going to become a nun.

I shyly confided this ambition to my favorite young nun, Sister Evaristo. She surprised me by advising against it. "My child," she said, "I have watched you carefully in two of our plays. I think the theater is where your future lies."

It was all I could do to keep from telling her the whole truth. Maybe she knew. I heard later that Sister Evarista was made to do penance for giving me such worldly advice.

When the school year ended, I went back to Mother in East Saint Louis, and Dorothy came on from Massillon to join us. We lived with our Uncle Harry, Aunt Rose, and Cousin Clay. But every morning both Dorothy and I went over to East Saint Louis to help Mother in the shop. Her little business was beginning to be profitable, and we loved living with our relatives. It was a happy time.

Next door to Mother's shop was a nickelodeon, a place for showing the earliest motion pictures. They had no sound. When we weren't busy in the shop, Dorothy and I would run next door.

The viewing hall was small, with rows of wooden chairs, a black upright piano, and a white sheet hanging in the front, where you might expect a stage. When the lady piano player struck the first chords, the lights went out. The camera projectionist turned a crank, and the flickering film's title would flash on the white sheet. We were off into a new and wonderful world of make-believe.

Usually the films took no longer than ten minutes each before THE

END flashed on the screen. A program was made up of three or four films. When the lights were switched on again, we'd be back in that dreary little room with an ordinary bedsheet at its front.

We had no idea that this entertainment we were seeing would soon mean the end of the traveling acting troupes and of a way of life that had supported us for so many years.

CHAPTER ELEVEN

We Meet an Old Friend

D. W. Griffith

During the autumn of 1910, I came down with typhoid fever and Mother's candy and ice-cream shop burned to the ground. There was no insurance and once again we were penniless. A sad year followed. Mother took a job in Springfield, Ohio, managing a confectionary and catering business. Dorothy and I went back to Massillon and Aunt Emily.

We had heard nothing from Father for a long while. Any thoughts of him had been stored away in the attic of my mind. But one day we got a letter from his older brother, Grant. Father was sick and confined to a sanatorium in Oklahoma.

Mother and I decided it was my duty to visit him. Train travel was nothing new to me, so I went out to Shawnee, Oklahoma, by myself and stayed with Uncle Grant and his family for several months. I hardly saw Father. He was too sick for company. Less than a year later he died.

The next spring I joined Mother in Springfield. This time Dorothy was away at a boarding school in West Virginia. We would pick her up there in June and continue on to New York City. After all, we were past the gawky stage; we were young ladies now. Perhaps we could return to the stage in grown-up parts.

On our way, we stopped in Baltimore to visit with some old friends, the Meixners. Mr. Meixner had been Father's partner in the ice-cream and confectioners' shop so long ago. We stayed with them for two weeks. One day Mr. Meixner gave all the children nickels to go to the moving pictures. Dorothy and I went to our second nickelodeon and saw a film called *Lena and the Geese.*

Except for the faint whir of the projector and the tinny piano accompaniment, the room was silent. We could see that we were in Holland. Lena, the peasant girl of the film's title, was pretty, with expressive eyes, a fetching smile, and masses of blond curls. What's more, she looked familiar.

"Lillian!" Dorothy whispered. "That's Gladys! Gladys Smith!"

She was right. It was our old friend Gladys. Excited by this discovery, yet fascinated by the story on the screen, we sat there. What a film it was, calculated to move the heart and exercise the tear ducts. We noticed that it was an American Biograph production. It was the longest film we had ever seen—fifteen minutes. After THE END flashed on the screen, we could hardly wait to get back to the Meixners'.

"Mother! Mother! Guess who we just saw acting in the flickers?" Dorothy shouted as soon as we were inside. "Gladys. Gladys Smith!"

Mother was shocked. Those of us who acted on the stage looked on film as an inferior sort of entertainment—a novelty, not an art form. "Oh my," Mother said sadly. "The Smiths must be having hard times." We decided to look them up when we got to New York. It would be good to see them all again.

When we reached the city, we rented a room in a boardinghouse on Central Park West. We assumed we would find Gladys Smith at the Biograph studio, so we took the trolley down to Fourteenth Street and easily found number Eleven East, a brownstone between Fifth Avenue and Union Square.

We stopped to read the sign in its window: AMERICAN MUTOSCOPE AND BIOGRAPH COMPANY. Inside, we found a winding staircase. At its right, there was a partition with a window in it, like a box office. A middle-aged man sat inside, whistling.

"Will you kindly let us see Gladys Smith?" Mother asked.

He looked blank. "No one here by that name."

"There has to be!" Dorothy spoke up. "We just saw her in one of your pictures, *Lena and Geese.*"

"Oh. You mean Little Mary. Wait a minute." He disappeared in back and before long returned with Gladys. She seemed more grown-up, her hair falling in ringlets to her shoulders. We hugged and kissed, then sat down on a bench and tried to catch up.

Although she was known in films as Little Mary, not only Gladys but all the Smiths had changed their last name, too. They were the Pickfords now.

"Mr. Belasco changed it when I was in *The Warrens of Virginia,*" she explained. "He thought Pickford sounded much better."

"Mr. Belasco?" I said in awe. "We're hoping to see him soon."

"I'm going to be in his new play this fall," Gladys/Mary said.

Dorothy wondered how she could be in a play and work in the movies at the same time.

"Oh, the movies are great between stage jobs," Mary said. "I've been in films for three years now, and all that time our family has been together. I make more money than ever before, too. Much more! We have a nice apartment, and Mother has her own car."

"A car!" Dorothy whispered incredulously. Was it possible that films offered such grand pay? Mary urged us to try the movies while we were looking for a play.

"Wait here and I'll get our director," she said.

Just then, a tall, slender man came down the stairs, singing. It was something from an Italian opera.

"Mr. Griffith," Mary called. "I'd like you to meet some old theater friends, Mrs. Gish and her daughters, Lillian and Dorothy."

To me, he looked like a giant. He had a large nose and a profile that belonged on a Roman coin. It was an important face, and he carried himself like a king. His gaze was intense. He seemed to be dissecting us. What I didn't know was that he needed two young girls for a new movie he had in mind.

"Where are you from?" he asked, looking at me.

"The theater," I said, "but we come from Massillon, Ohio."

"Massillyoon," he said mockingly. "Well, I could tell you were Yankees the minute I saw you." Then he turned, smiling, to Mother. "Can they act?"

Before Mother could reply, Dorothy interrupted with outraged dignity, "Sir, we are of the *legitimate* theater!"

"Oh, I don't mean just reading lines," he said. "We don't deal in words here." Seeing our confusion, he said, "Come upstairs to my rehearsal room, and I'll soon find out." He started up the stairs, then called down, "Miss Mary, will you please send Mr.

Barrymore, Mr. Booth, Mr. Walthall, and Bobby up to me."

Dorothy and I obediently followed him. We were frightened, but we felt that the place couldn't be all that bad if our friend Gladys—Mary!—and a Barrymore were part of it.

Mr. Griffith led us into a large room that might once have been the master bedroom of the house. Soon several young men came in. He explained that we were about to rehearse the story of two sisters trapped in an isolated house. Four thieves are trying to get in and rob their father's safe. He stared at us. "You aren't twins, are you? I can't tell you apart."

He strode from the room and came back with two ribbons, one red, the other blue. "Tie these on: blue for Lillian, red for Dorothy. Now, Red, you hear strange noises. Run to your sister. Blue, you're scared, too. Look toward me, where the camera is. Show your fear.

"You hear something. What is it? You're two frightened children, trapped in a lonely house by these brutes. They're right in the next room! Blue, you hear the door breaking. Run in panic—quick. Try to bolt it—"

"Wh-what door?" I stammered.

"Right there in front of you! I know there's no door, but pretend there is. Run to the telephone. Start to use it. You realize the wires have been cut. Tell the camera what you feel. Fear—more fear! Look into the lens! Now you see a gun coming through the hole. Look scared, I tell you."

It wasn't hard to obey. We were practically paralyzed with fright.

"No, that's not enough! Girls, hold each other. Cower in that corner." Whereupon he pulled a real gun from his pocket and began

to chase us around the room, shooting it. We didn't know he was aiming at the ceiling.

"He's gone mad!" I thought as we scurried around the room, frantically looking for a way out.

Suddenly, everything was quiet. Mr. Griffith lay down his gun. He smiled broadly, evidently pleased with the results. "That's a wonderful scene," he said. "You have expressive bodies. I can use you. Would you like to make the picture we've just been rehearsing? It's called *The Unseen Enemy.*"

Our ears still ringing with the pistol shots, Dorothy and I were struck dumb. On stage we would have known just what was to happen next. We'd have learned our lines; we'd have known the whole story before we ever began acting. Here there was no script. Mr. Griffith was making it all up; he was the only one who spoke.

"Well—" I began. "We'll have to ask Mother. Actually, we are looking for parts on the stage."

"That's all right," he said. "I can't use you every day, so you'll have lots of time to call on agencies. Would you care to start today as extras, sitting in on an audience scene? I can use all three of you."

We asked Mother, who thanked him and said, "Yes."

Such was our introduction to working in the movies, and to David Wark Griffith and his style of directing. We were paid five dollars a day, whether we played leading roles or were extras. In just four days we earned forty-five dollars, more than we had ever earned for that same amount of time in the theater.

We left our names, asking to be called whenever there was work.

CHAPTER TWELVE

Flying On Broadway, Landing in Hollywood

Lillian in *The Good Little Devil*

We looked on the movies only as a way of feeding and sheltering ourselves until we got back on the stage. We heard that David Belasco needed several young actresses for a forthcoming production, *The Good Little Devil.* So we looked up an old friend from touring days who was now Mr. Belasco's manager.

He arranged an interview. We knew we were lucky. There were hundreds of applicants for each role.

We went to Mr. Belasco's office above the theater that bore his name. Now that we were growing up, Mother decided not to accompany us.

Mr. Belasco, a handsome man with thick white hair, sat behind his desk as we walked timidly into the room. It was midsummer, and the office furniture was draped in white dust sheets. The blinds were drawn against the heat. I tried to avoid Mr. Belasco's stare by slipping behind Dorothy.

I was the elder, but I was petrified. Then Dorothy slithered behind me. We kept up this ridiculous shuffling, one behind the other, until we had nearly backed out of the office. Mr. Belasco just watched.

"Thank you," he said softly, at last, "for letting me see what you look like from the last row. Now come closer, please. I don't bite."

We obeyed.

"I'm sorry I can't use you both," he said. "I need just one more actress." Then, pointing to me, he added, "You can play the Golden Fairy. Do you like flying?"

I could hardly breathe. "Yes, sir. I love flying."

"Have you ever tried it?" he asked.

"No, sir."

Whereupon he hired me.

When we brought the news home to Mother, she said, "I wonder if this is the play Mary is in?" It was! She and Ernest Truex were its stars.

Meanwhile, since neither Mother nor Dorothy had a part for the fall season, we continued to drop by Biograph for any work it could give us. There was never a script to study, no lines to memorize. Everything seemed to spring magically from Mr. Griffith's brain.

Dorothy and I were so wary of the film business that first summer that we asked Mother to come with us to the studio each day.

As I knew I would soon be going into rehearsals for *The Good Little Devil,* I told Mr. Griffith.

"How much is Belasco paying you?" he asked.

"Twenty-five dollars a week," I said with pride.

"Well, stay with me and I'll pay you fifty dollars a week to be a permanent member of my company."

I didn't know what to say to this grand offer.

"However," Mr. Griffith went on, "you'd be very foolish to take me up on it. The name Belasco is worth ten times my offer."

He added that his offer would stand, if ever I decided to accept it. Furthermore, he was going to take Dorothy with him to California on a fifteen-dollar-a-week minimum guarantee. Five dollars would be added for each day she worked!

So, once again, we were all to separate. Dorothy, aged fourteen, would go to California. Mother decided to return to her job in Springfield, Ohio. And I, almost sixteen, would tour in *The Good Little Devil* and come, at last, to Broadway with it.

Rehearsals with Mr. Belasco were yet another new experience. So much time was spent perfecting every single word. I had trouble with *apple.* It was important that the audience in the gallery hear those two *p*'s. I was swallowing them. It took me weeks to get it just right!

Next came the lighting. Each fairy had a tiny spotlight placed low, to illuminate the face. Mr. Belasco wanted the audience to see our eyes. So there was a strange new stage direction. Wherever I went, I seemed to hear, "Hit her with the baby!"

I was Morgan, the golden fairy, and I flew across the stage suspended from a half-dozen wires. These were manipulated from backstage by eighteen strong German rope-handlers. Because I said I loved flying, I was chosen to do the wire testing for all the fairies. I had to be in the theater extra-early before each performance.

In Baltimore, during the Christmas matinee, I had an accident in the second act. While the stage was darkened, I flew down from a great height to a five-foot wall. There I was to rest a moment in the spotlight. Then, protected by the wires, I would fly across the entire stage. Instead, a wire came loose from the clasp on my back and I stepped off the wall into space. It was a six-foot drop to the stage. Worse, the audience laughed as I fell. Possibly I was more shocked than hurt, but when I heard the laughter, I was certain I had ruined Mr. Belasco's play.

He happened to be in the audience that afternoon and came backstage to comfort me—and to find out whether or not I was badly hurt. I wasn't.

He was pleased with me as the gold fairy. The newspapers quoted him as saying I was "the most beautiful blonde in the world."

At our New York opening everything went smoothly. The critics praised *The Good Little Devil* and we settled in for a long run.

Like a grownup, I took a small room at the Marlton Hotel on Eighth Street. I bought a little Sterno stove so that I could warm my food. Mostly I ate eggs, baked beans, and tea. Not much of an improvement over the oatmeal and milk diet my first year on the road! Now I was hoping to save at least ten dollars each week to send to Mother.

Whether it was my dreary diet, the long working hours, or the toll taken by my stage fall, I got steadily thinner and paler. Mr. Belasco grew concerned. He asked Mrs. Pickford to take me south for a couple of weeks' rest, hoping that the sun would restore me. She couldn't leave her own children. Finally, he offered to send me to California, where Mother had by now joined Dorothy. He promised me my understudy would play the role only until I got stronger, but everyone in the cast doubted I would ever return.

Mr. Belasco paid my train fare. The eighteen men who worked the wires were so upset at my departure that they brought a small brass band to the station to give me a grand send-off.

I was overwhelmed by Mr. Belasco's generosity. Later the stage manager told us that Mr. Belasco was afraid of a lawsuit because of my fall. Such an action had never occurred to us. Our family didn't know how to sue anybody.

I left for the West in a flood of affection and got to Los Angeles in February 1913. The city smelled like one big orange grove. The temperature was warm and welcoming.

Mother hurried me off to a doctor who was afraid I might have pernicious anemia. He prescribed a simple program for recovery: sunshine, rest, good food, and, for a tonic, a California red wine called Zinfandel. I had to drink two big tumblers of it every day!

When I felt better, as I did surprisingly quickly, Mr. Griffith kept his word. He put me to work on the terms he had offered in New York. With Dorothy's pay and Mother's bit-part money, we could afford a nice comfortable apartment. Soon we exchanged it for an even nicer, more comfortable bungalow.

One morning I woke up and realized that here we were—all together at last. We had the house I had dreamed about years before as a small traveling player. We were warm. We could afford good food, lots of books, and nice clothes. Mother didn't have to worry one bit about money anymore. Everything we had ever wanted as children now was ours. It was like a fairy tale: "And they lived happily ever after." We wondered if we would.

ABOUT THE AUTHORS

LILLIAN GISH is truly a legend in her own time. As a young girl in the early days of movies, she became a star, the leading lady of such D.W. Griffith classics as *Birth of a Nation* (the first feature-length film), and her career continued successfully into the talkies. On Broadway, in the 1930s, she played Ophelia to John Gielgud's Hamlet. Most recently she appeared in *Sweet Liberty* with Alan Alda. To date, she has appeared in over a hundred films and fifty plays. In 1984, Miss Gish received the American Film Institute's coveted Lifetime Service Award for her extraordinary contributions to the industry.

SELMA G. LANES, a highly esteemed critic and reviewer of children's books, is the author of *The Art of Maurice Sendak* and *Down the Rabbit Hole: Adventures and Misadventures in the Realm of Children's Literature.* As a child, she first heard of Lillian Gish from her mother, who at age nine had seen the star in *Birth of a Nation* and never forgot the experience.

The photographs in AN ACTOR'S LIFE FOR ME were provided by Lillian Gish. Many are in the collection of the Library of Congress.